KT-362-234

For the children of
St Christopher's School,
Staverton, Devon
- P.B.

For Finn, Samuel
and Amelie
- P.D.

First published 2014 by Macmillan Children's Books
a division of Macmillan Publishers Limited
20 New Wharf Road, London N1 9RR
Basingstoke and Oxford
Associated companies throughout the world
www.panmacmillan.com

ISBN: 978-0-230-76679-2 (HB)
ISBN: 978-1-4472-2343-6 (PB)

Text copyright © Peter Bently 2014
Illustrations copyright © Penny Dann 2014
Moral rights asserted.

All rights reserved. No part of this publication may be reproduced, stored
in or introduced into a retrieval system, or transmitted, in any form,
or by any means (electronic, mechanical, photocopying, recording or
otherwise) without the prior written permission of the publisher.

Any person who does any unauthorized act in relation to this publication
may be liable to criminal prosecution and civil claims for damages.

1 3 5 7 9 8 6 4 2

A CIP catalogue record for this book is available from
the British Library.

Printed in China

C015817926

PETER BENTLY   PENNY DANN

POLLY PARROT PICKS a PIRATE

MACMILLAN CHILDREN'S BOOKS

Polly the parrot was sick of her tree.
"Same old branches and leaves, same old nothing to see!
Same cheeky chimps with their same cheeky tricks –
I'm fed up with living out here in the sticks!"

She squawked, "It's a life on the ocean for me!
I'll find a pet pirate and sail off to sea.
I'll find one who's clever and dashing and brave,
Who's handsome and clean and who won't misbehave."

So off fluttered Polly that very same day
To the inn by the harbour at Buccaneer Bay.
There sat the pirates with all of their crews,
"Now," wondered Polly, "which one shall I choose?"

Bartholomew Blood appeared smart at first sight,
But sadly for Polly he wasn't too bright.
"I can't find my treasure!" he said with a frown.
"You noodle!" squawked Polly. "Your map's upside down!"

"Oh dear," Polly sighed, "but I won't give up yet.
I'm sure I can find a much cleverer pet!"

Phineas Mudd seemed a fine fearless sort,
But was really the clumsiest pirate in port.
He swung from the rigging with daring and dash –

Then slipped on a barrel,

and CRASH!

and KER-SPLASH!

"Oh dear," Polly sighed, "but I won't give up yet.
I'm sure I can find a less bumbling pet!"

Crazy Kit Cutlass looked fearsome and brave,

Till he ran with a screech from the Smuggler's Cave.

As Crazy Kit trembled in terror beside her,
Polly peeped in and discovered . . .

a spider!

"Oh dear," Polly sighed, "but I won't give up yet.
I'm sure I can find a less cowardly pet!"

She searched the whole harbour, she flew all around,
But the perfect pet pirate just couldn't be found.

Gentleman Ned
was too fond of his clothes,

Two-Tooth Trelawny
kept picking his nose,

Mad Dog Domingo wore stockings that stank,

And Jack Salamander kept walking the plank.

Sighed Polly, "I can't find the pirate for me,
So it looks like I'll have to go back to my tree."

She was just heading home when she heard a man say,
"There's a big pirate battle in Buccaneer Bay!
Redbeard is fighting with old Pegleg Pete,
They're the very best pirates in all of the fleet!"

"At last!" Polly thought, as she turned for the sea,
"They sound like the perfect pet pirates for me!"

SMASH! went the pirates

and WALLOP!

and CRUNCH!

They fought all day long (with a short break for lunch).

"Surrender!" cried Pegleg, but Redbeard roared "Never!
Surrender yourself! I'm the best pirate ever!"

Redbeard and Pegleg were in a right strop,
They battled and bashed until Polly squawked,

"STOP!"

"The way this is going there won't be a winner,
Except for the sharks, who'll have pirates for dinner!

Why don't you stop fighting and simply agree
That you're BOTH the best pirates who sail on the sea?"

Then Polly looked closely and saw a strange thing,
That massive red beard – was it tied on with string?

She tugged at the beard, and it fell in the sea!

"Great galleons!" gasped Pegleg. "Old Redbeard's a . . .

"SHE!"

"Do you know," chuckled Redbeard, "this parrot is right,
There's really no need to continue our fight."

"Why don't we join forces?" said Pegleg. "With pleasure!
Double the pirates means . . .

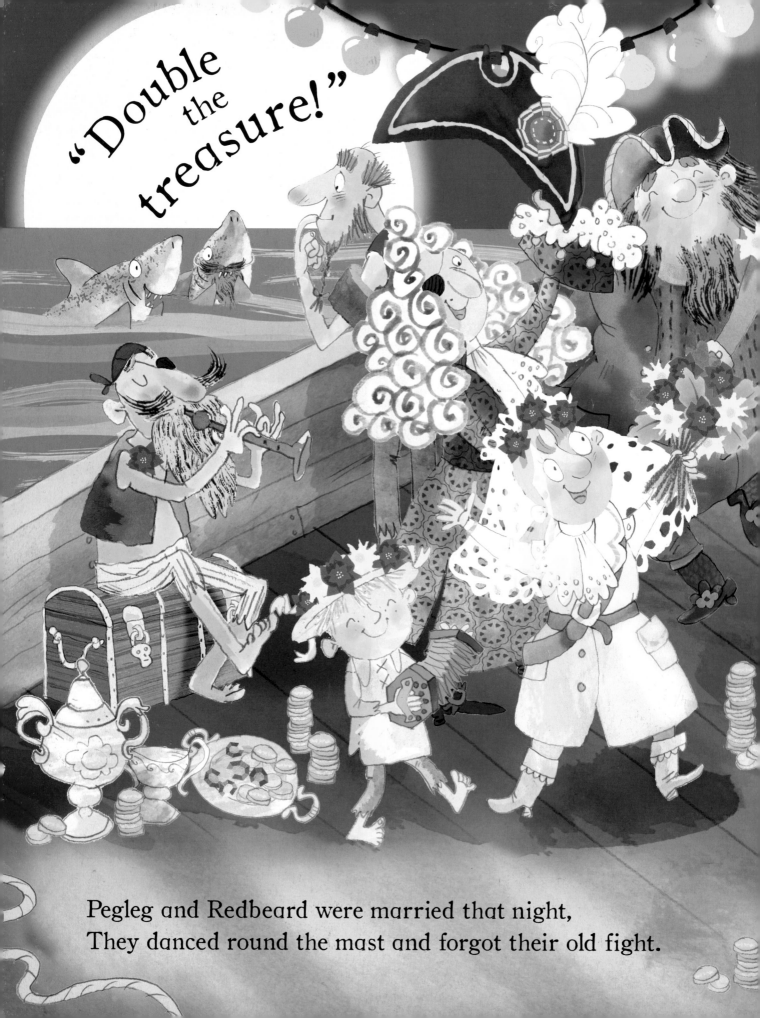

"Double the treasure!"

Pegleg and Redbeard were married that night,
They danced round the mast and forgot their old fight.

"Hooray!" Polly cried. "What a fabulous do!
I wanted one pirate and now I've got two!
They're clever and dashing and fearless and brave
(But I might have to check that they don't misbehave)."

So with her new pets Polly sailed off to sea,
And she thought, "It's a life on the ocean for me!"
As she turned to her tree for one last farewell glimpse,
She laughed, "Now I'm finally free of those chimps!"